THE DARK SECRET

"THE EXPERIMENT"

PART 1

D. J. BRAND

To order additional copy of this book, contact:

2708 Armidale Road Blaxland's Creek New South Wales Australia

+1 347 878 1961/+612 8006 0204

info@shrubspublishing.com

"The Dark Secret of Ian's Peak: I have created the world's most powerful experiment, Dream Reality." Whoever enters this experiment will see things that have already happened, happening, or yet to happen in a vision or a dream."

Professor Lynx

1892

Prologue

*S*trangers don't usually pass through the town of Ian's Peak, and when they do, the whole town knows about it. During the hot summer month of January while all of the children were still on their Christmas break, a stranger was passing through; noticing no one was around, there was no motor vehicle or movement whatsoever.

"Where is everyone?" he thought to himself, but really couldn't give a damn.

He was out to do a job and wasn't going to leave until the job was completed. The unknown stranger wore a black leather jacket, pants, and gloves, and was quite tall with a solid build, someone you wouldn't like to meet in a dark passage. He walked through the town with only the sound of his own footsteps. The high school that he headed towards was becoming clearer in the distance. He remembered the school well, and the memories that he was having for just a split second just frightened the hell out of him; but deep down he knew that it will be over in just a few seconds, He was holding a can of kerosene; this unknown figure seemed to be dangerous and looked quite angry at the world and had planned to do something that is horrible and mad. The evil tormented face said that he was up to no good and something bad was going to happen tonight.

Lindsay Peterson had been the principal of Ian's Peak High School for Twenty years, and before that, he even went to the high school himself as a student. Now he was not only the principal of this high school but his fourteen-year-old daughter Sam Peterson was also going to the same school. This time of year, is bad for the principal, especially before the beginning of the year, when he had to organized and be ready for next week when school goes back into motion. The yearly planner for the coming year has always been the first thing that Mr. Peterson checks to make sure that everything is in order and there is nothing out of place. The school had its ups and downs in all the years of teaching and still manages to continue. A noise from outside distracted him; that caused him to stop working and look up towards the window. What he saw was shadows in the distance, and suddenly the strange feeling become stranger than before, as if someone had just walked over his grave. The shadow moved from tree to tree, and at first, he thought that he was imagining it all and continued back to work.

This outlander of Ian's peak was standing outside the school grounds, and now he knew exactly what to do. The memory that had entered his mind was a bad memory, and Mr. Peterson was in it; this bastard principal, and then he'd shook it off almost as quick as it appeared. The stranger picked up the full can of kerosene and started pouring it around the school grounds.

Mr. Peterson could smell something burning and could hear crackling of fire that didn't seem to be too far away; the smell was strong and horrible like some sort of chemical. He thought that he would go and investigate it and there was no way that he could possibly knew what was going to happen next. When he looked out the window into the darkness, he saw something terrifying, something he'd never seen in all the years of teaching, his worst nightmare coming true, fire, and it was heading straight for him. Mr. Peterson fell back as he moved away from the window; he tried to get to the door to escape, but it was too late. The school was burning like a piece of wood in a fireplace. Lindsay was trapped knowing that he'll never see daylight again.

The stranger sneaked off into the darkness, as if he'd never been there in the first place, waiting to see what happens when morning came.

Chapter One

"James Thompson, it's time to get up," said the voice that was disturbing the nightmare I was having. Everything was fading before my eyes, the school, the fire, Mr. Peterson, and even the stranger. My eyelid slowly opened, and Mary Thompson stood over me wearing her nurses' uniform. It took me a few seconds before I realized where I was and this woman standing over me was…

"Mum," I said, "what time is it?"

"It's almost nine o'clock," she replied. "You'll be late for work."

Like a normal teenager, I wasn't listening to Mum. My mind was still in the nightmare I had just minutes ago of the high school burning down, and caused the death of Mr. Peterson, the principal of Ian's Peak High School. He was trapped inside with no way out; it seemed so real, as if I was there. I felt the heat of the flames and remembered the look on the principal's face when the devilish fire confronted him. That's impossible; it was only a dream, but I had dreams like this before, only to find out that all the events that happened in the dream did happen. I remembered the one I had only a few years ago so clearly when Dad died. He was out chopping down trees for his work contract when suddenly one of them fell back and landed right on top of him, killing him instantly. The night before that dreadful day, I had dreamt about it and tried to warn him not to go to work and that something bad is going to happen to him. He wouldn't listen, and still went out and did what he had to do to support his family. Dad turned around to Mum that day said the normal everyday goodbye and then to me as if he was going to see us again. Both my parents thought I was crazy, but I knew I wasn't. Things like that only happen since we discovered Cave Death.

I've never believed in the stories our parents told us. I always have thought about entering the cave during the school holidays 4 years ago in 2018, I was only 10 at the time and curious about the cave. I entered the cave with one of my best friends Josh Brown. I have known him all my life, and unlike me he'd believed in the stories that's going around. It took me a long time to convince him otherwise. When I did finally persuade him to come along, he thought I was crazy. He didn't mention it at the time, but we were friends for such a long time, I could read him like a book; the expression on his face said, "Are you crazy? What if our parents find out?"

***

One fine Saturday morning, we were out on the adventure of a lifetime. We were riding our bikes up to the cave and parked just beside it.

"It looks just like any other cave," I thought to myself.

I have never been this excited before. I jumped off my bike and quickly gathered my belongings together. Josh, on the other hand, wasn't as excited as I was. When Josh arrived, he just sat on his bike for a few seconds longer and stared at the cave. He didn't want to move any closer because of the legend that he'd heard about a few years ago.

"Do we have to?" Josh asked.

"Of course, we have to!" I said,

"But it looks so creepy." Josh said.

"You're not going to chicken out on me now, are you?"

"What about the legend our parents warned us about?" Josh said,

"What did I tell you before?" I asked, but then continued before Josh had a chance to answer.

"The legend was made up by our parents, because they didn't want us to enter the cave."

"Well, is that so bad?" Josh nervously asked.

"Look," I said, starting to lose my patience, "Just get off that bike and follow me." He knew he wouldn't win this argument, so like a follower, Josh got off his bike and gathered his belongings together. I was carrying a torch ready for when we entered the dark cave. I was in front of Josh for the whole journey and managed to jump over a big hole that I saw in the ground. Josh wasn't so fortunate; he didn't see the hole and stepped right onto it, and fell into a big pit; there was a big thump as he hit the bottom.

"Josh!" I screamed while running to the edge of the hole. I looked down but couldn't see him anywhere because of the darkness.

"Josh!" I called again, and this time I heard murmur, which sounded like coming from far, far below into the darkness.

"Hang on, Josh," I called as loud as my lungs could carry, "I won't be long."

I had a feeling that we might need some rope for our journey, which I was carrying across my shoulders. I eased the long rope down the deep hole, tied the other end around the nearest tree stump, and slowly climbed down. When I reached the bottom, I turned on the torch to look around for Josh. He was lying on the ground, unaware of what had just happened. Josh tried to get up but couldn't because he'd sprained his right ankle.

"Don't move," I said, "I'll see if I can find something to support you."

I shone the torch around and couldn't believe what I had just discovered, corridors in all directions.

"Wow," I said.

"What?" Josh asked, but really didn't care much, and just was thinking about the pain that was causing him.

"I'm not sure, but I think we are actually inside Cave Death."

"You're kidding."

"No, I'm not. Just wait here, I'm going to check it out," I said while walking in the direction of one of the corridors.

"Okay, just don't be too long. This place gives me the creeps."

"I won't," I said while following one of the corridors and becoming increasingly excited about this discovery I'd come across. I managed to find a branch for Josh to use as a walking stick. At first, when he tried to get to his feet, he couldn't bear the pain; when he did finally get to his feet, we walked in a slow pace to the other side of the corridor. It felt as if we were walking for hours or even days. When we made it to the other side, Josh was ecstatic with the discover that I'd come across. We found a strange-looking door with no handles and an inscription that read, *Dream Reality*.

"I wonder what that means," I said.

We looked around for more clues to the inscription and a way of opening the door. I had my notebook, so I wrote down the inscription. Josh found a way to open the door, there was a strange-looking button under a rock, that he'd decided to push. The door opened like the door of an elevator. We saw what looked like a laboratory, as described by Mary Shelley in her *Frankenstein* classic. There was a long rusty bench with buttons, and levers and switches were on the wall.

"I wonder what happened here," Josh said, with great curiosity.

"I'm not sure," I replied, "but I would love to find out."

We entered the room to look around and I went straight to the bench to inspect it. Josh wandered over to have a closer look at the buttons and levers. The machine looked so old and dusty, as if it had sat there for hundreds of years. I thought I could have a bit of fun by lying down on the bench. There was a head piece connected with wires to the machine. I manage to put it on for my amusement.

"Hey, look at me," I said, "I'm Frankenstein's monster."

"Get off that thing." Josh said, sounding concerned and worried. "You don't know how dangerous this thing could be."

"Relax, will you?" I said, looking at Josh. "I know what I'm doing, and besides, this thing looks harmless enough."

"I don't know James." Josh replied.

I also noticed there are straps attached to the bench that goes around the body.

"Just strap me up will you!" I said,

"I don't like this, James."

Josh strapped me down to the bench, so I couldn't move at all.

"Arghhh," I growled, moving around like a monster, which startled Josh and he starting to move backwards.

I didn't listen to Josh, whom I should have, so I continued messing around playing Frankenstein. Suddenly, Josh fell back and hit one of the levers by accident, and it slipped down to the "On" position. Electricity came from the bench and through my body and I thought I been struck by lightning. Josh panicked to shut down the power to save my life and he managed to turn of the machine, but it took him a few minutes. I was very lucky; the electricity died down almost as quick as it begun. My body went limp, and for a minute I thought I was dead. Then, I heard Josh's voice from a great distance.

"James!" he screamed, "Please, God! No!"

I started to cough and felt sick. I felt like I'd been hit by a truck or something much worse. The earth started to shake and everything around us begun to collapse. Josh quickly unstraps me.

"Quick, James," Josh said, becoming frantic now. I managed to get to my feet, but they gave way and I fell to the ground again. Josh helped me back *onto my feet. We grabbed our belongings and headed for the entrance and home. It took us a while before we found the entrance, but we found it. We were glad to see daylight again. When we made it as far away as possible, I couldn't stand any longer and fell to the ground just in time to watch the cave collapse. I had a feeling it wouldn't be our last adventure, and I was sure Josh was thinking the very same thing.*

"James Thompson, are you listening to me?"

I could hear Mum in the distance while coming out of the memory that I was having.

"What?" I replied.

"Oh, never mind, just get ready for work!"

During the holidays I manage to get a part time job at Ian's Peak Hospital, as a cleaner for extra money. My mobile phone was ringing for a few seconds; when I looked down, I could see that it was "Sam Peterson", the daughter of the principal that appeared in my nightmare last night. I had a feeling I wasn't going to like this phone call very much.

"Hey, Sam," I said.

"Hi, James," Sam replied, but I did notice the anxiety in her voice.

"What's wrong?" I finally asked, but deep down I had a sick feeling of what she was going to say and I really wasn't looking forward to the answer to see that I was right and the dream wasn't just a dream.

There was no answer for a few seconds. Sam had never gone this quiet on the phone before, not once that I could ever recall. At first, I thought it could be my mobile phone because I have lost reception before a few times.

"Are you still there?" I asked.

"Yeah, I'm here, she said. "It's Dad. He died last night. He was working late at school when a fire broke out."

It was my turn to go silent, I knew what she was going to say, because I had seen the whole thing as if I was there, and realistically when you think about it, I was.

"James," she continued, "they said it was accidental death."

I knew how she felt. I had lost my dad only a few years ago. I still didn't know what to say to her. What could you say to your girlfriend, when you had seen what happened that night in a dream and there was nothing you could do about it, except just hope it wasn't real. One thing I could say though, it was no accident, and someone had done it deliberately: but why?

What had Sam's dad ever done to him?

With a bit of luck, we'll find out the truth. How could I tell Sam that I had a dream about it all happening while it was happening? She would think I've gone mad, like my parents did, because sometimes I think I've lost my mind too.

"I'm sorry, Sam," I managed to say. "Do you want me to come over today?"

"I thought you'll be working!"

"I'll tell mum what happened. I'm sure she'll understand."

"That would be great, James."

"I'll see you outside the school grounds in half an hour."

"Sure, I'll see you then."

I press the red button on the mobile phone to end the call and looked around the empty room with a creepy sensation. What's going on here?

Why am I dreaming reality again?

Is it something to do with Cave Death?

Maybe is some sort of coincidence, but one hell of one.

Chapter Two

S am Peterson was waiting for me just outside the school grounds, well what was left of it anyway. She's a year younger than me, and we'd met when she started her first year of high school. Sam is one of the most popular girls at school; the guys are envious and jealous of me because we've been going together now for just over six months. She has long blonde hair and is very slim with a tanned complexion. On my way to the school grounds, I couldn't believe this had happened, and the worst thing about it, that I had dreamt of this disaster last night, but couldn't warn anyone. It could be my fault when you really think about it. Sam was in the far distance when I arrived, and I rode my bike up to her. She looked so different; I've never seen her like this before. I knew what she was feeling, the same way I was feeling when I lost my dad. I got off my bike and put my arms around her to show her how sorry I am and gave her light kiss on the cheeks; I felt her relaxing in my arms.

"Oh, James," she said, "why did he have to work last night?"

"I know, Sam, but you can't turn back the clock."

"That's what I keep telling myself," she said, feeling hurt from what had happened. "He was in his office when the fire broke out. Just now they found some sign that it could be arson and that someone had deliberately set fire to the school."

"Let's go for a walk," I said, taking Sam's hand and slowly heading towards the park. "there's something I've been meaning to tell you."

"What?" Sam curiously asked.

"Come on, let's go and sit down."

When we sat down on the bench at the park, I spotted Josh and waved to him to try and get his attention. He entered the cave with me a few years earlier, but I've never told him about the powers that I'd gained from the experiment. Maybe it's about time he knew the truth. Josh is bigger than I am, and he always enjoys gaming online, and likes going on the internet. I managed to get his attention and he headed straight for us.

"Have you seen the school?" Josh asked with excitement. Josh noticed Sam was upset, "What's wrong?"

"Her dad passed away last night," I replied. "He was working late when the fire broke out."

"Oh, Sam, I'm sorry." Josh managed to say.

"That's alright Josh," Sam replied, "You didn't know."

Sam turned back to me and asked, "Now, what is it you were going to tell me?"

"If it's private," Josh said, "I can come back later."

"There's something I've been meaning to tell both of you for such a long time." I said.

"Well?" Sam asked, feeling more anxious than ever.

"Last night, while I was asleep," I said, "I had a dream of the school fire. It felt real, and when I woke up, I was burning up like I was on fire myself."

"What?" Sam said. "In your dream, did you see Dad?";

"Yes," I replied, "your dad was working late, like you said earlier. He went to the window because he heard a noise coming from outside. He looked out the window and could see the fire coming towards him. He couldn't make it out on time."

"James, it's only a dream, it couldn't be real." Josh said.

"That's what I kept telling myself this morning", I replied, "until Sam rang and told me what had happened. When she told me that they'd found some evidence that it was arson, then I knew it wasn't just a dream."

"What are you talking about?" Sam wanted to know.

"It wasn't just an accident; it was deliberately lit by someone that came into town. A Stranger, who I've never seen before in my life."

"How can you have dreams like this?" Sam curiously asked.

"This wasn't the first dream I had that had happened in real life." I replied.

"Did you have others?" Sam asked.

"When Dad tragically died, I dreamt about that dreadful accident the night before and tried to warn him. He wouldn't listen to me and thought I was imagining it all and went out to work anyway, then he was killed by a falling tree, the same way I predicted."

I went quiet, walked over to a tree feeling disturbed about the whole thing. Sam came up behind me and put her arms around my waist from behind to give me a slight hug.

"Something seems to be bothering you," she said.

"Josh, do you remember when we entered Cave Death few years ago?" I asked.

"The cave with a legend so no kids would enter," Josh replied, "we entered anyway, what's that got to do with now and this?"

"We entered a room, which looked like a laboratory set from a horror movie. I laid down on this strange-looking bench, and by accident you fell back onto one of the levers on the wall, which activated the machine. I was electrocuted badly; I knew then how Frankenstein monster must have felt like."

"Like I said before, what's that got to do with the dream you had last night?" Josh wanted to know.

"Well, I happened to study up on the history of Ian's Peak a few months ago and found out something interesting about Cave Death."

"What did you find out?" Josh asked.

"Apparently during the late 1800s, a Professor Lynx did some strange experiment deep in a cave close by, called Dream Reality. Everyone in town thought he was a crazy evil old man. He claimed to have seen vision of true events that will happen in the future."

"You think you were caught up in this experiment and you too can see vision of the future?" Sam curiously asked.

"Yeah, sounds crazy now that you put it like that." I replied.

"Okay, what happened in the dream you had last night?" Sam wanted to know.

"Someone came to the school, poured kerosene all around the school grounds, and lit a match to it. Before you knew it the whole school went up in smoke."

"Did you manage to get a good look at him?" Josh asked.

"Unfortunately, I did, he looked a shocker. He's enough to give anyone nightmares."

"Why don't you give the description to the police?" Josh wanted to know.

"Are you kidding? They would want to know how I got that information."

"James's right," Sam said, "the police would think he's crazy if he told them the truth. We have to deal with it ourselves."

"What are you talking about?" I wanted to know.

"We got to find out who the stranger is and then go to the police."

"No, it's far too dangerous," I replied.

"Come on, we've got to get him for what he's done." Sam said.

"Just let the police handle it."

"The police haven't got a good description and probably don't know where to start."

'Sam's right." Josh said.

I looked at Josh and Sam. Sam has a look, a pleading look, a look I can't for the life of me resist.

"Okay." I finally said.

"Great," Sam said, "I knew you would help."

I was wondering for the rest of the day, and night too, whether I was doing this for Sam to find the murderer of her dad or whether I was doing it for myself to find out the answer to 'Dream Reality'. I was still thinking about it that night until I fell into a deep sleep.

Chapter

Three

*T*he stranger has come back once again to the small town of Ian's Peak,
driving around the streets, taking all the back roads in his silver
Commodore so no residents could see him. He parked his car in a good
hiding place where no one would ever think to look. He walked the rest of the
way to the park, where he walked a mile or two, until he could see the park
ahead of him.

The Park seems to be hiding in the back of his memory, a memory he'd
tried to forget, but couldn't. In the memory there were kids hanging around the
park and playing the evil game of football.

"Only sinners play football!" he remembered his mum bellow out.

"These kids are sinners and will never make it to heaven because of
the game they are playing!"

The stranger was not there sixteen years later to preach about football
or anything else. He was here for revenge on something he remembered that

happened over a decade ago. He recognized Josh Brown as one of the kids at the park, who is the spitting image of his father Jack. The other kid, who is younger than Josh, must be his brother Paul. The stranger been watching Paul for a few days now. He decided to get his revenge on Jack by taking something that belonged to him. Jack had taken something from him as a child, like his sanity, his girl, and his life. The stranger just has to pick the right moment before he makes his move. The football came right to where he was standing. Josh had kicked it too far; Paul came running for the ball and when he was about to pick it up, he noticed someone standing there. Paul looked up and saw a man standing only a few feet away, someone he'd never seen before. The stranger bend down and picked up the ball for Paul.

"Hi kid." The stranger said smiling at the youngster.

"Who are you?" Paul wanted to know.

The stranger looked out towards Josh and noticed he was talking to a blonde-haired girl. He knew Josh was just a fraction out of range and that he could do what he had come to do.

"An old friend of your father," the stranger said, "I'm in town on business for a few days, and your dad asked me to get you."

"Why?" Paul asked curiously.

"Your mum is very sick," the stranger said, "and he needs you home as soon as possible."

The stranger noticed that Josh has gone off a little further down the road with this girl he'd noticed earlier.

"What about Josh?" Paul wanted to know.

"Josh have already gone. I have just seen him leave." The stranger lied.

Paul looked back and couldn't see Josh anywhere.

Could this stranger be telling the truth?

Is Mum really sick?

Why did Josh go and leave him all alone?

I suppose it should be all right if Dad said so.

"Okay." Paul said.

"That's a good boy." The stranger said smiling.

Josh came back after the girl left. He had missed Paul by a few seconds. He noticed his younger brother wasn't anywhere in sight and ran to where he had last kicked the ball. He found the football, but no Paul. He screamed out loudly.

The buzzer went off. Everything in my mind came to a halt and started to fade away before my eyes, and I was coming back to reality again.

The alarm woke me from another nightmare. I was sweating like water running from a tap. I reached over to grab my towel from the side cupboard and wiped the sweat of my forehead. My mind wasn't clear at first, and then I started to remember about the dream I just had. It came to me slowly at first but eventually came to me in complete picture. I turned off my alarm and looked at it for a good few second more. I just managed to read the digits. It had just turned eight in the morning. I still saw the stranger whom Paul was abducted by.

"Josh," I said to myself, "I have to warn him if it's not too late."

I picked up my mobile phone, which was near my bed, and was going to ring Josh's mobile, but as I touched mine another vision came, just before Josh and his brother left for the park; Josh put his mobile on his bed and forgot to take it with him, so I knew it was pointless ringing him on his mobile. Then I rang his home number instead, and the phone on the other end rang a few times.

"Come on Josh," I whispered to myself, "answer the god damn phone."

Someone answered the phone; it was Josh's mum. Anne Brown sounded as if she had just woken up.

"Hello," she said, "Brown's residence."

"Hi, Mrs. Brown, it's James," I said. "Is Josh home?"

"No, I'm sorry. You just missed him James," Anne said, "Josh has taken Paul to the park."

"Thanks," I replied, "I catch him there."

"Have you tried his mobile phone?" Anne said.

"No," I replied, "he left it on his bed and forgot to take it with him."

"Ok," she said, as she hung up the hand piece.

"He left on his bed." Anne thought to herself, "How on Earth did he know that."

I'd quickly pressed the red button on the phone to end the call. Paul is in trouble. I have to warn them. Just hope it's not too late. I picked up my coat and left through the back way.

***

Josh kicked the football to his younger brother Paul, who managed to mark it quite well. He's not bad at playing football for a nine-year-old. Now Paul has the ball, he kicked it back to Josh. Next time when he kicked the ball, he didn't notice where he kicked it or how far it went. Josh was too busy noticing this blonde-haired girl Susan McGregor, who had just moved from Scotland only a few months ago. Josh always wanted to ask her out ever since she'd moved to Ian's Peak, but never had the courage. He didn't think that she knew he existed, until today. After he had kicked the football, he stopped to talk to her, forgetting everything else, even playing football with his brother. He did notice that I was riding down one of the streets, waving my arms about, yelling something out to him, but he couldn't put his finger on it. Josh went a little bit closer to see what I wanted. Unaware of what was happening with Paul, I stopped my bike as close to Josh as possible, trying to control my breathing so I can get my breath back.

"It's Paul!" I exclaimed. "Don't leave him alone!"

"What are you talking about?" Josh wanted to know, worried with my sudden outburst.

"Just trust me," I said. "Where's Paul?"

"He's over there," Josh replied, pointing in the direction where Paul was a few minutes ago, but realized he was nowhere in sight and started running in that direction. I jumped off my bike and ran after Josh. What Josh found was only the football, and there was no sight of Paul anywhere. When we couldn't find young Paul, Josh fell to the ground and screamed with rage. I knelt down beside him.

"That's what I've been trying to tell you," I said, "I had another dream last night. I think it could be the same guy that burnt down the school. When I tried to ring you, I had just missed you."

"What am I going to do?" Josh wanted to know.

I couldn't answer him straight away, but deep down I knew I can't answer him at all.

"Mum and Dad are going to kill me!" Josh said.

"I'm sure it won't be as bad as all that."

"You wanna bet, Dad went nuts for losing his best golf ball," Josh said. "You think he will pat me on the back for losing his son?"

"I guess not," I said. "Come on, we better call the police."

We got on our bikes and rode off down the street to let Josh's parents know so they could call Ian's Peak police department.

Chapter

four

"YOU WHAT?" Jack demanded, while his face was burning red with anger.

"We were playing football," Josh said, "and all of a sudden he just disappeared."

"He couldn't have disappeared just like that!" his father replied with anger and frustration that went through his entire body all at once. Josh and I were waiting for his body to explode. Anne was sitting on the lounge and trying to be calm herself with the situation, but she found it wasn't easy.

"Calm down." She managed to say.

"CALM DOWN!" he exclaimed. "I don't know how you can be so calm when our young son is out there with some sort of a mad man!"

"It's no good blaming anyone." She replied.

I managed to take a look at Josh's eyes; he got the look of anger, desperation, and hate building up,. He turned around and headed for his bedroom, trying not to show anyone how hurt he was feeling about this whole predicament.

"Look, Mr. Brown," I said, "I was there, and it wasn't Josh's fault."

Jack just had to sit down; everything that was happening seemed to be too much in one day.

"Look," I said, "I know where Paul was last seen and maybe, just maybe there could be a clue on his whereabouts."

"James's got a point," Anne said. "Why don't the both of you go to the park and look around?"

"Okay," Jack finally agreed, "then I better go and speak to Officer Butler."

When we made it to the park, we looked around for any clues leading up to the disappearance of young Paul. They didn't seem to have much luck, but because of my Dream Reality powers, I seemed to remember where the car was hiding before Paul disappeared. He went straight to the spot and found some clues of a car being parked there, a place where no one would ever think to park a car. Why would they?

"Look here!" I called out to Jack, who came over almost immediately to see what I had found. There were tire tracks marked in the ground. I touched the marks slightly and something came to mind, a car, a silver commodore that I had seen parked here in my dream earlier that morning. I could see the license plate number and tried to concentrate on the numbers, which read XLV221. I repeated the numbers to Jack, who just looked at me with curiosity.

"What?" Jack wanted to know.

"It's silver Commodore with a license plate number XLV221."

"How did you know that?"

"No time to explain. Call Officer Butler to see who owns the car."

Jack took out his mobile phone and pressed the digits to Ian's Peak police department. He waited a few seconds before someone answered.

"Yes," Jack said, "could I speak to Officer Butler please."

Officer Bill Butler had been with Ian's Peak police department for twenty years. He knew Jack when he was a kid, always on the wrong side of the law, until Officer Butler gave him a good talking to. Jack remembered an incident that happened during high school when he was a teenager, involving another disturbed kid, Wayne Cassidy, who went berserk and end up in an asylum before the end of the night. Wayne probably still there. Bill Butler was the officer who was on duty that night, radioed out to the school. When the officer found out Jack Brown was behind it, he wasn't surprised at all, because of Jack's background. He'd never finished his schooling and had left during year ten. It wasn't until Jack married Anne, and become pregnant with his child, they named the new-born Joshua. Jack then becomes more responsible and found a decent job so that he could support the family. Josh was then born that changed Jack completely and turned him into a sensible young man.

"Officer Butler here," the voice said over the phone. Jack shook of his thoughts as quick as it came.

"Bill, it's Jack."

"Jack, what's the matter?" the officer asked.

"It's Paul, he's vanished!" Jack replied.

"What do you mean vanished?" Bill wanted to know.

"Josh was playing football down the park, and when he turned his back Paul had disappeared."

"Where are you now?"

"I'm over at the park at the moment," Jack replied.

"I'll meet you there, and I think we may need to organize a search party."

"Great, Bill. There's something else, I've got a feeling he's been abducted."

"Are you sure?" Bill asked.

"We found a bit of evidence," Jack said. "James seems to remember seeing a silver Commodore in the area with a license plate number XLV 221."

"Okay, I check it out, and I can be at the park within ten minutes."

Jack hung up the mobile phone leaving Bill with the information I had originally given him in the first place. There was something else that disturbed me.

Something I could see happening. Something, which won't be in the future, something that happened a long time ago, I just couldn't put my finger on. I have shaken of the vision almost as quick as it had begun. Jack looked at me with concern and curiosity all at once.

"Are you okay?" Jack wanted to know.

"What?" I asked.

"What happened?"

"Nothing!" I replied.

Jack wasn't sure it was nothing. He knew something had happened to me. I just didn't seem to be myself today. What happened all those years ago?

Whatever it was, I got a feeling I will find out very soon.

Officer Butler organized the team of guys to search for Paul. Jack knew the guys since high school, and they were almost as concerned about this happening in Ian's Peak. A child had never been abducted in this town before. Why now?

Nobody seemed to know the answer.

Officer Butler decided to spend the afternoon with Jack and Anne while he still waited around for the phone call about the silver Commodore and the owner. While waiting for the call, Bill had another talk with the two boys about the sudden disappearance of Paul. We told him everything that he already knew. The only thing I didn't tell him was the fact that I had been in an experiment that had given me the power of Dream Reality, making me see things happening before they actually happened. I didn't want anyone to think I've gone crazy.

Everyone and their dogs were out searching for Paul. Sam came over to keep Josh and me company. Sam was upset about what was happening, especially since what happened to her dad and the school two nights ago. After Officer Butler left for the day, I couldn't help wondering about the dream I had the same morning it had happened. Why couldn't I get there sooner? I couldn't help to think I could be held responsible. Stop talking crazy, I kept on telling myself. I tried to warn Josh, but it was too late. I decided to leave Josh and Sam behind and got out and join the search party. I advised Josh not to come and thought Sam could stay with him. I didn't like the thought of leaving Josh on his own. We searched everywhere for Paul. Houses, sheds, behind shops, and even the bushlands. Not even one clue of his whereabouts.

**

"They have searched for hours now," Josh said. "Why haven't they found anything yet?"

"Don't worry, they will," Sam replied.

"You don't suppose he could be ..." he started to say but couldn't finish the sentence. Sam knew exactly what he was talking about.

"No, of course not," she assured him.

"I can't help thinking it's all my fault. If anything happens to him, I'll never forgive myself."

"Look it's nobody's fault except for the person who abducted him." Sam said. "Why don't you get some sleep? You might feel better when you have a good night sleep."

"I doubt it."

Officer Butler was starting to suspect that Paul was no longer in Ian's Peak but didn't like to say anything to Jack at this stage. We searched everywhere and there was still no sign. No one will give in and assured the family that the search would continue until we find something.

"Find something?" Josh replied. "What do they mean find something? Are they expecting to find his body?"

I kept telling him to have a positive outlook, but it didn't matter what I said, Josh couldn't help but keep seeing his brother in a small coffin; he quickly shook off the thought.

Chapter five

T he morning was very slow for Anne; she couldn't sleep a wink worrying about her son out there in this hot night, not knowing what dreadful things could have happened to him. She tried not to think about it or she would break down and cry. Who could be doing this to us?

Nobody knew the answer to any of the questions she asked. Someone out there knew the answer. Unaware of what was happening outside, the stranger all dressed in black, wearing gloves, and holding an envelope, walked up to the Browns' letter box. He dropped the envelope in the box and sneaked away quickly. Later that day, Jack went out to the letter box to see if they had any mail, and when he got there, he noticed there was an envelope that had been hand-delivered. He looked at the envelope with curiosity before entering the house. Anne was waiting for him in the lounge room. When he entered the house, she looked at him and noticed a worried look upon his face.

"What's wrong?" Anne asked.

"This letter," Jack said. "It looked like it's been hand-delivered."

"Who by?"

"I'm not sure," he said. Jack opened the envelope, read what was inside and fell into the nearest chair beside him.

"What is it?" she asked curiously. Jack handed Anne the letter, and she looked at it for a few seconds.

"Your son is here today, gone tomorrow," she reads, "Oh, Jack." She burst into tears.

"Don't worry," Jack said, putting his arm around his wife. "We'll just hand this letter to Bill straight away."

"What happens if it's too late?" she wanted to know.

"Stop thinking like that," he said.

"We have got to be realistic," she replied. "We may never see our boy again."

"Don't do this to yourself."

Jack looked at the letter once more. Something about the letter seemed familiar. What could possibly be the connections?

He started to think and remembered something to do with the past when he was around Josh's age.

"Your son is here today, gone tomorrow."

Mary had said something similar to him many years ago. Something about what Wayne had told her just after he betrayed and murdered his baby brother, like Cain did to Abel in Genesis of the Holy Bible.

"Your brother is here today, gone tomorrow," Mary told Jack all those years ago and then shook off the thought with a fright, like someone had walked over his grave.

The phone suddenly rang, which startled both Anne and Jack, but he stared at the phone for a few seconds, which was sitting on the corner cabinet of the lounge room, then he answered it.

"Hello," he said.

"Jack, it's Bill"

"Bill, have you got news about the owner of the car?"

"I have, and I don't think you're going to like it."

"Just give me the worst."

"Okay, embrace yourself," the officer said. "The description of the car and the number plate was owned by Wayne Morton."

"We don't know any Wayne Morton."

"I did more checking up. Morton isn't his real name or doesn't exist, he'd changed it and get this, his real name is Cassidy, Wayne Cassidy."

"My God!" Jack said.

"I'm sorry Jack, Wayne Cassidy has escaped from the asylum a few days ago, bought this car, and was heading straight up here."

"To get his revenge I suppose."

"I guess that's his plan after what happened in School sixteen years ago." Bill replied.

"there's something else." Jack Said.

"What?" Bill curiously asked.

"We received a letter that someone dropped in our letter box," Jack said as he starting to read the letter to Bill, "your sons here today, gone tomorrow."

"Do you think Wayne dropped it in your letter box?"

"I do now, it all starting to make sense. Wayne said something similar to Mary when he'd murdered his brother."

"I'm going to look around for this car and any clues. The search party is still on."

"Thanks Bill."

Jack hangs up the phone and looked at Anne. He looked confused and worried.

"Well?" Anne asked.

"We think it could be Crazy Wayne." Jack replied.

"Crazy Wayne?"

"Yeah. Do you remember the kid in high school that Mary went out with?"

"What? Why is he doing this after all these years?" Anne asked.

"We think it could be revenge after what we did to him back then."

Could it be possible that Wayne Cassidy is responsible for the abduction of their son Paul and perhaps the murder of Lindsay Peterson and guilty of arson? How could they let Wayne just walked out of the asylum like that?

Anne looked up at Jack with even deeper concern, because now there's a motive. After all, they were responsible for what happened to Wayne all those years ago. Anne's best friend Mary had nightmares for years after the incident. She fell pregnant with Jamie all because she'd wanted to forget about that night that had ruined her life. Mary was planning to study as a lawyer, not a nurse, but she'd left school early to look after her child, without regrets though.

"I better let Mary know what's happening and to watch out for Wayne." Anne finally said.

"Yeah, I think that's a good idea." Jack replied.

Chapter

Six

It had been hours since Anne phoned Mary about the past and Wayne. Mary was sitting on one of the lounge chairs looking through an old photo album. There was one photo of Mary when she was younger with her arms around a good-looking young man. When they were in primary school, all the girls were asking him out at the time. It wasn't until they were in High School that Mary started going out with the young lad in the photo. She turned the photo over to read a message that he'd written on the back, 'to my sugar pie. Love Wayne.' She reads quietly to herself. Tears started to roll down her cheeks. Mary was in her dressing gown and was lying on the couch and starting to remember what happened the night of the dance. She had blocked it out for years because it was a terrifying experience.

"Why Wayne? Why are you doing this?"

"Don't worry, sugar pie," she could hear him say, "everything will work out for the best."

"Come on Wayne, let's play on the swings" she could hear her say when she was younger.

"I love you, my sugar pie," Wayne said.

"I love you too," she replied.

Mary shook off her thoughts with the door slamming shut. It was only me that startled her, and she dropped the photo album to the floor. Wayne's photo slipped out, and I knelt down to pick it up for her, when I noticed one photo in particular and the face looks familiar.

Who could it be?

This mystery person was embracing Mum; I've seen him somewhere before, much older than he is in the photo.

"Mum, who's this?" I asked.

"No one," she replied.

"It's him, isn't it?" I wanted to know, starting to catch on.

"He's the one that has kidnapped Paul, isn't he?"

"I don't know what you are talking about."

I was holding on to the photo, and the visions were coming to me.

"Baby Killer, baby killer, you killed your own brother." He heard voices of children.

"Baby killer," I repeated what I heard.

"I don't know what you are talking about," she said and was shocked and amazed that I knew what happened in her past.

Then I started to see more of the vision. I still held the photo tight, and mum looked at me with concern. She didn't know what to do but wait. Then the vision came in complete picture, what had happened over a decade ago ....

Chapter Seven

*T*he vision started with someone lying in a hospital bed after giving birth to a beautiful baby boy, who she'd name Greg. "Gregory Lloyd Cassidy," she said.

She sounded pleased with herself for naming the baby after her father, who had tragically died in an automobile accident a year ago. This would be the boy to remember him by. She had a thirteen-year-old son also, who came in to visit her and his newborn brat baby brother. He was Wayne Cassidy, and his own mother always believed he was the son of the devil. She tried warning people of Ian's Peak who thought she was crazy and never listen to her. Wayne was a small kid, and the other kids bullied him, except for one girl, Mary Dobson, who was a year younger than Wayne and whom he liked very much. Baby Greg spoiled everything; ever since he was born, Wayne always seemed to be in trouble, even though half the time he didn't do anything. He always got the blame just the same.

"*Wayne Cassidy!*" *his mother would call out to him,* "*you come here this very instant.*"

He would run and hide for the rest of the day. When he finally decided to go home, his mother would hit him across the face so hard it left a red handprint on his cheek.

"*No, Mother,*" *the boy cried.*

"*Lies! Always lying!*" *she exclaimed.*

"*No, Mother! I'm telling the truth!*"

She grabbed the nearest thing, which happened to be a frying pan that was simmering on the stove, and Wayne saw how red hot the pan was.

"*You know what happens to naughty little sinners? God will punish them!*"

"*No!*" *he screamed.* "*Please, No!*"

"*Turn around and bend over!*" *she bellows at him.*

"*Please, Mother!*"

"*I said turn around now!*" *she shrieked even louder.*

Wayne had no choice but to turn around. She threw him against a bench ripped off his jeans, and holding the pan and using it with all of her force, she hit him so hard across his bare backside that Wayne screamed out in agony. The new born woke up crying.

"Look what you've done! You've woken the baby!" she said. "You make me sick. Now go to your room, and I don't want to see you for the rest of the night."

Wayne rushed out of the room. He threw himself onto his bed and couldn't help but cry out louder than the baby itself. Hours passed and Wayne was still lying on the bed listening to see whether he could hear his mother or even the little devil's child. The only sound he heard was the rhythm of his mother and that pathetic little baby brother sleeping.

"If it wasn't for him," he thought to himself, "I wouldn't get hit like I did tonight."

Wayne slowly got up from his bed, still sore from the red-hot pan hitting him. He couldn't put on his pants because of the pain and agony that was going through his body. He managed to wipe away the tears from his eyes. He couldn't care if he was parading around the house with no clothes on, better still, the streets; maybe the neighbors might see all the marks on the lower part of his body and then realized what sort of beatings he had to put up with. He slowly got up and walked towards the door. Wayne listened closely for any noise, and there wasn't any. He peeped out and saw the room his brat brother was lying in. He slowly opened the door and crept in, and there was his brother, Little Gregory, the devil's son himself, who should be sent back to hell, where he belonged.

"I must destroy him and send him back to hell," he thought to himself. Wayne walked over to him and looked at him sleeping peacefully, pretending to be innocent, like butter wouldn't melt in his mouth. "How pathetic," he thought, disgusted about the way the baby was acting. Wayne could hear his own heartbeat racing. He knelt down to pick up a pillow and slowly put the pillow on young Greg's face and put all his force on that pillow.

The next day at school, Mary was very sympathetic towards Wayne for the loss of his brother. They said it was cot death that happened to Gregory, which was very common for newborn babies. Wayne looked different. He didn't look like his usual self. He was like another person, like he was a victim of the body snatchers or something, but that was impossible.

"Are you all right?" Mary finally asked.

"Why shouldn't I be?"

"I don't know. You don't seem to be yourself today."

"How do you want me to act like?"

"I don't know," she said. "I suppose it's normal after the loss of your baby brother."

"Loss of my baby brother!" Wayne said laughing out loud. "Loss of my baby brother! That's a good one."

"It's not meant to be a joke," she said.

"I'm sorry, I thought it was," he replied. "I'm glad the little brat's dead."

"That's terrible thing to say," she said, looking more concerned than ever.

"Is it?" he said, laughing even louder. "I killed him with these hands."

"What?"

"You heard me."

Mary starting to get scared, backing away slowly from him, shaking her head.

"NO!" She screamed out.

"It's true, Mary. I've sent my brother back to hell where he'd belong," he replied. "My brother's here today, gone tomorrow."

Wayne slowly walked closer to Mary, who backed away even further.

"Everything's going to be all right," he said.

"Keep away from me!" she screamed.

She ran off still hearing Wayne laughing wickedly. Mary kept on running. She didn't know what to do about Wayne. Mary knew Jack's house wasn't far from her now. She had to tell someone. After all, Jack is a close friend, and he might even know what to do.

Mary ran to the door of Jack's house and knocked loudly. Jack answered the door looking concerned.

"What is it, Mary?" Jack wanted to know.

"It's Wayne. He ...." She started but couldn't finished the sentence.

"He what, Mary?"

"He said something dreadful to me. I think he needs help."

Mary explained to Jack what Wayne had just told her earlier and the look that he had given her, not to mention the wicked laugh like he didn't even care about anything. Jack couldn't believe what he was hearing. He had never liked Wayne much. He always believed Wayne was a strange kid, and the whole family seemed to be weird. It comes from the parents and the upbringing. Good thing young Greg did die, or he would have become like the rest of them.

"Don't worry," Jack said, grinning to himself. "Leave him to me, I'll work out what to do."

Before too long, every kid in Ian's Peak High School knew about it, and they were talking about it behind Wayne's back and laughing at him. They called him "Baby murderer."

They wouldn't dare say it to his face. Mary was not impressed about what they said about Wayne. She had thought that Jack would help him, that's why she had gone to him in the first place. The kids couldn't wait for the night of the school dance. Jack has planned something horrible with the whole school, except for Mary, because he knew she wouldn't be part of it.

Mum was watching me with deep concern. I was still holding the photograph of Wayne, and I went into a rage.

"James, what's wrong?" she asked.

I couldn't answer her. I couldn't even hear her. My mind was still in the past. I kept seeing the school and the other kids. Some of the kids I knew as grown-ups. There were Josh's parents and even Sam's dad Lindsay Peterson. He was the principal even back then over a decade ago. Mum had to hold tight hoping I would snap out of it soon enough. I had to continue with the past to see what else happened. I had to know what went on back then so I could get some answers about what's happening now and why it's happening. So, I concentrated once again, to know more of the night, the night that ended up in tragedy, the night that could have started the whole mess of what's happening today, the night of the dance ....

***

The night of the dance came along, and Jack had a plan to get back at Wayne. There was Jack Brown, Anne Peters, and Jamie Thompson. Jamie married Mary after she became pregnant to try to forget about this night. They had a baby boy and they name him James Cedrick Thompson.

The school dance is only one night of the year that all the kids hang around together as one big group. Tonight, seemed different. There was tension in the air. They were all dancing to all sort of music.

Tainted Love came on the stereo, and Mary grabbed Wayne by the hand and pulled him up onto the dance floor.

"Come on," She said, "This is my favourite song."

"Don't touch me please," the song went on, "I cannot stand the way you tease."

Jack went up to his friends in the hall.

"It's time," he said.

The kids started to leave the hall one by one, until the only ones are left were Mary and Wayne, who were still dancing. Mr. Peterson was still in the hall. He wasn't even paying any attention to what was happening. The song ended and it was Mary who noticed that everyone had left the room.

"Where are they? Where is everyone?" she asked curiously.

"How the hell should I know!" Wayne snapped.

She looked around and couldn't see anyone. Then Wayne heard noises coming from outside.

"Wayne .... Wayne," the unidentified voice said.

"What's that?" Mary asked.

"Let's go and have a look," Wayne replied.

They went outside. Wayne could see fire at the back of the school. They continued on towards the fire which burned furiously. Something is odd, but neither Wayne nor Mary could put their finger on it. The fire kept on burning. Wayne could see something ahead of them. He saw a white figure with what looked like a pair of horns on its head. The devil himself came back to haunt him, but why?

He gave him the gift that he requested, his baby brother.

"Wayne," the figure spoke.

"What do you want?" Wayne asked.

"You have killed me and sent me down below."

"Gregory?" Wayne asked curiously.

"Wayne, you have been a bad boy," The figure said smiling to himself.

"It wasn't my fault. You got to believe me."

"Believe you!" the figure exclaimed.

"You have driven me to it," Wayne said, sounding more pleased with himself.

"If it wasn't for you, I would still be in my cot!"

Wayne fell to his knees. Mary realized what was really happening. The kids were playing a joke on him, but why?

Why play a terrible prank on someone? What has he ever done to them?

Mary started to walk backwards slowly because she didn't want to be part of this set up, it had gone far enough. She looked back to the hall and could see Mr. Peterson at the dance just watching from the window. He was not doing anything to help Wayne. The other students were teasing Wayne, and all Mr. Peterson could only do was watch, probably having a good chuckle himself. Wayne started hugging his knees tight, sniffling, and crying. The other kids gathered around Wayne and started to laugh and giggle. Mary couldn't believe how mean her friends were.

"Stop it!" she demanded.

No one paid any attention to her. Why would they?

Wayne shouldn't be at their school. He was a nutcase and shouldn't even be on the streets. The kids were still tormenting him by chanting, "Baby Killer, baby killer."

Wayne looked up and saw the face behind the mask. It was Jack Brown. His mind was on Jack's face and he would never forget that look as long as he live. Jack picked up a can of kerosene and poured it in a circle around Wayne, then lit a match that started to burn furiously around him. He looked scared and desperate.

Why shouldn't he?

Mary pushed past the kids to get to the fire; she'd managed to grab hold of Wayne's hand to drag him out of the fire to a safe place. Wayne went berserk; he started throwing things around the school ground. Mr. Peterson came out of the school with a straitjacket that he'd found in a cupboard from the school doctor's clinic to place around him until the ambulance arrived. They took Wayne away for a very long time.

***

I finally pulled myself out of the past, and I was glad it didn't freak me out. Mum was still sitting on the lounge noticing the sweat running down my face like running water from a tap.

"Are you okay?" Mum wanted to know.

"I don't know," I replied.

"What happened?"

"I saw what happened at the school dance all those years ago between this Wayne and Josh's dad."

"What?"

"I can't explain. The school dance and the joke the others played on Wayne."

"Yes, well, I'm trying to forget. We think he could be the guy who abducted Paul," she said.

"That's the only thing that does make sense," I replied.

I went to go out the front door when Mum stopped me.

"Where are you going?" she wanted to know.

"I need to see Josh and perhaps his father. The jigsaw is slowly putting itself together."

I left to go over to see Josh. Could there really be a connection?

That's the only thing that does make sense around here. The fire, the school burning down, the abduction of Paul Brown, which happened to be one of Jack's kids, the ringleader of that terrible night. The sad thing about it is my dad's involvement as well.

Chapter
Eight

The people of Ian's Peak were still searching for Paul. The day turned into night, and there was still no sign of the boy. Officer Butler starting to suspect that he's no longer in Ian's Peak. All the houses had been searched. Every shed and even the bushlands had been thoroughly checked and still no sign. There wasn't even a clue. Anne couldn't take the search much longer; she felt like she would collapse, and Jack had to send her home to their place. When she got home, her head pounded with a migraine. And been thumping for hours, like someone was sitting inside her head with a sledgehammer banging against her skull. She just wanted to scream for help. Josh came out of his bedroom, with me following not far behind him. She didn't look too good because her lack of sleep.

"Are you okay, Mum?" Josh asked.

Just before Anne came home, I had managed to fill Josh in about the vision I had earlier that happened at the school over a decade ago: his dad being the ringleader and the rest of Ian's Peak being in on it. I had explained about the joke they played on Wayne Cassidy and how he went out with my mum during the school years. Wayne was taken away to an asylum. I thought Josh was handling it well, considering.

"I'll be fine," his mum said. She couldn't even open her eyes to look at us two boys because of the migraine she was having.

"I'm going out for a while to help with the search."

"It's almost dark," Anne replied. "They probably will be finishing soon."

"Don't worry, we won't be long."

"Okay, just be careful."

Josh and I left his mum to rest. They weren't sure about what to do next or where to search for Paul. When the boys left, Anne went upstairs to take a long bath in the tub to ease the pain. The phone rang, but Anne didn't hear it ringing because of the noise of the running water and the door being closed. The answering machine answered the phone for her.

"This is the residence of the Browns' household," said Jack's voice on the machine. "So, if you'd like to leave your name and number after the beep, we will get back to you as soon as possible, beep!"

"How do you like it?" said the caller. "It's not fun, is it, having something missing from your life. I've got your boy right with me. Say hello to your mummy!"

"Mum! Help me, please!" Paul pleaded out over the phone. "I can't see anything, it's dark, please come and get me."

The stranger grabbed the phone of Paul.

"So, you thought you got away with it, did you?"

Then he hangs up, but Anne didn't hear her son pleading for her, instead she was lying in the tub trying to ease the headache she had all afternoon. She was hoping they would find Paul soon. She still thought the same thing when she fell into a deep sleep.

We went over to Sam's place so she could join us. Josh and Sam were trying to think about where to look that no one even thought about.

Something came to me in a vision. A dark place, Paul strapped down to an old and rusty bench. Wayne was also there, lighting a match and blowing it out.

There was something about that place. It looked familiar. The metal bench with button, and switches and levers on the wall. James suddenly remembered where Paul could possibly be.

"Cave Death," I said louder than I thought.

"What?" Sam asked with curiosity.

"That's where Paul is, Cave Death."

"Of course," Josh replied, "that's one place no one would think to look."

"Okay, we go to my place," I said, "I'll tell Mum I'm staying over your house tonight. We pick up a few things then head off to the cave."

"I'll give Mum a ring to let her know what's happening. I hope it's not too late."

There was another vision, which I didn't let the others know. It was too wild. It was a fire, an evil act of violence, and an explosion in Cave Death, and my mum was involved somehow. I shook off the vision almost as quick as it came.

***

Anne Brown woke up suddenly after she'd almost fallen under the water. Her migraine had eased off a little bit. She got out of the tub, grabbed a towel, and wrapped it around herself. When she got to her bedroom, she looked at the clock, which read three o'clock in the morning. The last time that she remembered, it was five o'clock in the evening, just after she'd come home from the search. Josh should be home in his bed; she did tell him not to be long last night. Anne decided to check on him. She went to Josh's bedroom. When she reached his room, something told her to look in Paul's room. So, she quickly had a look: nothing had been moved and the bed had not even been made; it was exactly the way he'd left it on the day he had disappeared. She went past the room to Josh's and opened the door to peep inside. The room was empty and there was no sign of her son.

Where could he be?

Josh had never been out this late before. Why wasn't he home?

Maybe Josh and James knew something about where Paul could be that no one else knew. Anne hurried to the lounge room to check just in case Josh was in the kitchen when she noticed the blinking of the light of her answering machine. She pressed the play button on the machine and heard Wayne's voice; he sounded as crazy as ever. Her son's pleading for help made tears roll down her cheeks. The beep came to show the message had finished. Another message came through. This time it was Josh.

"Mum," he said, "when you get this message, I hope it's not too late. We think we know where Paul could be, Cave Death. We are heading there right now. I've got James and Sam with me."

He then hung up with no more words or messages. Anne looked at the machine when the phone rang again, which startled her. She could only stare at the phone for a few seconds before answering it. Just in case it's Wayne again. But she took her chance and answered it anyway.

"Hello," she said quite startled, but she was relieved when it wasn't Wayne's voice, but Officer Butler's.

"Anne," Bill said, "I'm just checking to see if James with you?"

"No, and Josh isn't here either."

Anne explained to the Officer about the phone calls and what was said, and when she had finished, Bill Butler finally spoke,

"I'm coming over to pick you up. We are going to organized a group of people to head over to Cave Death as soon as possible."

Chapter

Nine

"Cave Death is just ahead of us," I thought, but was a little nervous about the idea of entering the cave again after what had happened last time. Unfortunately, I knew what was going to happen because of my Dream Reality powers that I encountered after this experiment that was left by Professor Lynx. When we arrived at the dark-looking cave, it didn't look any different than it did back then. Josh didn't move from where he was standing and just looked at the cave.

"I didn't think we would ever see this cave again," Josh said.

"That makes two of us." I replied.

"It looks creepy." Sam said with concern.

We went around the cave and prepared for almost anything tonight. Luckily, we thought to bring a few bits and pieces for the journey including a torch.

"Are we ever going to get out of here alive?" I thought to myself, still remembering the vision I had with Wayne of setting the cave on fire and the three of us on the other side of the flames. Mum was there too. She's going to get there just in time, but I don't know whether anything's going to happen afterwards. I looked around to Josh and Sam. I can't read their minds but I'm sure they are thinking the same thing I am. We came across a deep-looking hole and looked down into the darkness but couldn't see anything. I picked up the rope to throw down like I did a few years earlier. I tested it to make sure the rope was strong enough.

"I'll go first," I said, easing myself down the long rope.

"Easy does it," I thought to myself.

When I made it to the bottom, I yelled back to the others. "It's safe to come down."

Sam was the next to climb down, making sure she was careful at doing it. Josh came down last and he slipped and almost fell. He was lucky that he hung on tight and finally made it to where we are. I turned on the torch and shone it around the dark cave once again.

"Nothing has changed," I said.

I seemed to remember which way we went when we visited it last time. There was another door, which I didn't remember coming across before. Maybe it leads to another room, but what room?

There could be a lot of answers beneath the door. I wanted to know more about the experiment that took place couple of centuries ago. We decided to enter the room, and we discovered an office. It had a wooden table, a chair, and a journal, which was marked on one particular page. I went up to the desk to have a closer look so I could read what was written on it. I just couldn't believe what I was reading. Sam entered not far behind me and could see me disturbed and excited at the same time.

"What is it?" she wanted to know.

"It's a journal left by the professor."

"Professor Lynx, the creator of Dream Reality?" Josh asked.

"That's him," I replied.

"What does it say?" Josh curiously wanted to know.

"Professor Lynx, 1892," I read and then continued, "the Dark Secret of Ian's Peak: I have discovered the world's most powerful experiment, 'Dream Reality'". Whoever enters this experiment will see things that have already happened, happening, or yet to happen in a vision or a dream. I had a dream of a young boy who will enter the world of Dream Reality and see wonderful things and bad things. Use the power wisely and beware. I think they have found me and are wanting to burn me at the stake, because I can see things that haven't happened yet, so I better go."

"Poor guy, I wondered what had happened?" Sam asked.

"I'm not sure," I said. "But I think he'll let me know all in good time." I took out my mobile phone and start taking pictures of what I just read in the journal. I started to look through the journal from the beginning of the book. I found something of some interest about the project called Dream Reality and when he first decided to start the experiment. He had claimed God had contacted him to build this machine, so someone out there could have this power of Dream Reality. He wanted someone to stop crimes from happening.

"I must be that someone," I thought to myself.

I continued looking through the journal and came across descriptions that we've known as a TV set, video recorder, and even a microwave oven.

"Look at these," I said to the others. Josh had to hurry along with interest. Josh had a good look at the sketches but couldn't believe his eyes. Not even in your wildest imagination back in 1892 could you ever think of descriptions like these.

"That's incredible." Josh said.

"He must have seen people watching TV in his dreams," I said, "and the next morning sketched it on a piece of paper."

I also came across a picture of someone hanging from a tree. The professor had seen a hanging in a dream. And right underneath the sketch it read: 'Professor's hanging tree.'

"He must have seen his own hanging." Josh said.

"I think you're right there, and probably was waiting for them." I replied.

"That must have been awful." Sam said.

I continued to read on, and taking pictures, "According to Professor Lynx, after admitting there is Dream Reality, I can see moving pictures on a box and a big plane in the air called a jumbo jet. The folks in Ian's Peak think I'm crazy and an evil old man. They think I should be hanged or burned at the stake."

"That's enough!" Sam demanded. "I don't want to hear anymore."

Something distracted Josh that he turned around in all directions.

"What's that?" he asked.

"What was what?" I wanted to know.

The sound came again, sounding like some shuffling noise and groaning coming from another room somewhere in the darken cave. It couldn't be far from where we were.

"That!" Josh said.

We hurried out of the room. I was leading the way. The sound seemed to be getting closer and closer when we came across the room where the sound was coming from. The room was dark; lucky I still had the torch on full power. We entered the room and shone the torch around until we came across movements in the far corner. When we got closer to it, we noticed it was Paul.

"Paul!" Josh screamed out.

Paul was strapped down to the bench like I was a few years ago, where the Dream Reality experiment came from. He was still wearing the same clothes that he was last seen in on the day he'd disappeared. Josh rushed to him. Paul was gagged and blindfolded. When we got closer to him, Paul freaked out. He didn't know who was there because he thought Wayne had come back.

"Paul, it's me," Josh said. Paul recognized his brother's voice. We removed the gag and then started to unstrapped him and got him to his feet.

"Josh, where's Mum?" Paul asked. He was so glad to see his brother again that he threw his arms around him to give him a big hug. For the first time in Josh's life, he didn't push him away and hugged him right back.

"It's all right, Paul. I'm here and so are James and Sam."

Suddenly another vision came to me, it was terrible and frightening. A fire was starting with the four of them stuck on the wrong side of the flames not knowing how to get out. Wayne was on the other side laughing and saying, "Burn, burn, burn!"

Then I came back to reality.

"Quick, we got to leave, now!" I said, "there's going to be a terrible fire."

"Did you see something?" Sam wanted to know.

"Yeah," I said, "quick, we better hurry."

Before I had another thought, I had another vision that I didn't understand. I smelt a strange odor, which smelt like kerosene. I turned around, and this figure standing in front of the doorway with no way to escape was Wayne Cassidy with long hair and broad shoulders, weighing probably about 150 pounds. His clothes style was something from the 1970s. His hands were as black as spade, and his face was grubby with dirt. He was holding a match and was ready to strike it. When he did, the whole cave could go up in smoke.

"Don't do it, Wayne!" he heard a voice from behind him. Wayne turned around startled and recognized the person who spoke, someone he liked all those years ago.

"Sugar Pie," he said.

"Wayne, put the match down, you don't want to harm them," Mary said.

"No!"

Another voice startled Wayne even more. It was the voice of his enemy, the kid who was the ringleader over a decade ago. It was the voice of Josh and Paul's father; it was the voice of Jack Brown.

"Put the match down!" he exclaimed. "It's me that you want, not the kids."

"Mary," Wayne said, "get him away from me." He went to light the match when Mary distracted him again.

"Wayne, easy does it. Jack is just leaving." She said, looking directly at Jack who wasn't going to budge.

"I hope you know what you're doing," Jack whispered to Mary. She nodded slowly so Wayne couldn't catch on what they were planning to do. Jack left the cave quietly, so did Officer Butler and the others. Mary was left all alone with Wayne and alongside the three kids.

"Wayne, just let these kids go," Mary pleaded with him.

"But, Sugar Pie, this is a game," he said.

"What sort of game?" Mary wanted to know.

"The three little pigs and I'm the big bad wolf."

"But there are four of them."

"I see what you are trying to do. You think I'm a fruitcake, don't you?"

"No, Wayne," she said. Wayne walked over to the other side of the cave mumbling to himself, "they say I'm evil. Do you think I don't know what they are saying?" He then said, "No, Mary, I'm not the evil one, it's you and them."

Mary signaled to the kids to leave the cave. Josh took Paul out first, who was slowly followed by Sam, and then I followed behind her. I turned to mum with concern.

"Will you be, okay?" I whispered, which Wayne overheard. He turned around and could see the kids nowhere in sight except for me, and I also walked out of the cave as fast as I could.

"You shouldn't have done that!" Wayne Screamed.

"They are only kids," Mary replied.

"You're like the others always against me."

"No, of course I'm not. I love you, Wayne," Mary said, "it doesn't have to be this way."

"Yes, it does," he said, picking up the kerosene can.

"I've always loved you, sugar pie."

He poured kerosene all over his body, holding a box of matches. Mary started to walk backwards slowly. She knew he was crazy; she could see it in his eyes that he was going to light the match, and she didn't want to be in the firing line.

"Wayne, don't please," she pleaded.

"Ashes to Ashes!" he said, then struck the match at the side of the box and lit it as if he was lighting a candle on a birthday cake. It was finally over for Wayne and the shocking past.

 Epilogue

It's been a few weeks since the incident at Cave Death with Wayne and Mum. We have started back at school after the long hot summer holidays. The school is still being repaired after the disaster with the fire. We have to catch the bus to the next town for school until they're finished repairing ours. Wayne blew himself up, and Mum's in hospital mainly because of shock and is due home soon.

"She was very lucky," I thought to myself.

I remember the incident. Mum fell out of the cave seconds before he'd destroyed himself. I remember the explosion which had blown the cave to bits and left nothing of it now. I remember seeing a figure I couldn't identify it at first that pushed Mum out of the cave. He was about five foot and wasn't wearing a shirt: his pants were torn by the ankles, and he was unshaven and had a beard like a hermit. When he got up, he looked at me; and smiled then faded like another dream. This figure seemed to be from another time. I've seen him before in my other dreams. Professor Lynx had come there that day to rescue my mum. He must have seen what was going to happen or he must have heard me screaming for help and decided to come from another time to help me out on this one. He knew Wayne was just too strong for me to handle.

I'm glad things are slowly getting back to normal, and we all can start living our lives again. We had the funeral for Sam's dad, Lindsay Peterson, just the other week. The whole town showed up to give their last and final respect to the principal. Sam's still has her mother with her, but won't be the same without her dad, and I can understand where she's coming from with losing a dad. Josh and

Paul seem to be much closer now, which I'd never thought would ever happen. I don't think Josh would ever let Paul out of his sight for the rest of their lives or maybe until Paul's big enough to look after and fight for himself. That's what something like kidnapping does to a family, bringing them closer. You don't realize what you got in life until you lose it or don't have it, even though it's for a short time, which is in Josh's case. With a bit of luck, something like this won't ever happen in Ian's Peak again, as for me I'm still battling on with keeping everyone together.

Mum being in hospital, I'm learning to defend and look after myself. I'm learning more and more about Dream Reality experiment. Even though that's the end of Cave Death, it won't be the end of my powers I have gained from the experiment. The only ones that know about the power is Josh, Sam, and of course myself. We've decided to use if for good and help people. I'm sitting on the bus on the way home from school, which was after 3 p.m., when something came to me in a vision, lasted only a few minutes, something very strange, something which I've never seen before since I've moved to Ian's Peak …

A Man in his late forties was sitting on the edge of a bed visiting an elderly lady. It looked like it could be a hospital. This man has no name or at this stage even a face, but all you can see is his moustache.

Where is this place?

Could it be Ian's Peak hospital? Only in time we can tell.

He was wearing a business suit and was carrying a briefcase, which indicated that he worked somewhere in Ian's Peak and has his own business, but it's hard to tell what business he was in. He said goodbye to the elderly woman in bed and gave her a kiss on the cheek before exiting out the door and down the corridor. There didn't seem to be anyone around, except for a cleaner polishing the floors who looked very busy and concerned about what he was doing. He went up to the elevator, and there were three of them in a row. He pressed the button to go down. The floor number on the side of the elevator read 6, which indicated that he was on the sixth floor, and he wanted to get down to maybe the first floor. He looked around while waiting for the elevator to arrive. The door of the elevator opened pretty quickly. He entered, which left him in the small box on his own. It's late at night, and he's got early shift in the morning. He's only got a few hours to sleep before he has to get up again for work. He noticed the button hasn't been pressed yet.

"That's funny," he thought to himself, "I'm sure I pressed the button."

So, he pressed it again and waited, and before his eyes, he noticed that the light of the button went off again.

"What's going on here?" he thought to himself.

He pressed it again, and this time all of the buttons turned on and off and went berserk. He had never ever seen that happen in all the time he had visited the hospital. He felt as if the elevator was going down faster than the normal speed.

"What's going on?" he asked himself again.

He couldn't bear the speed that the elevator was going at, so he fell to the ground and huddled in the corner. His heart was racing at a hundred miles an hour. He curled up like a ball, waiting to see what was going to happen next. He thought that someone had messed around with the elevator and cut it so it would fall.

Suddenly, without any warning whatsoever, the elevator crashed to the bottom with a big thud. For a few minutes, he thought that he was unconscious and then he became conscious again without realising where he was or what had happened. The door of the elevator opened much quicker as it had closed. There was something that didn't make any sense at all. It looked cloudy outside like there wasn't an outside. He got to the edge of the elevator to see what was going on and who or what was out there. He couldn't believe it. His mouth opened wider than anyone could imagine, and he was ready to scream the most terrifying scream that anyone could possibly scream, so his mouth opened and out came...

The Dream Continues.....

Coming soon in 2023

The Dark Secret of Ian's Peak

"The Basement"

Part 2

Men have disappeared from the elevator of Ian's Peak Hospital. What happened to them? The biggest and most dangerous mission for James Thompson, who has the Dream Reality powers. Will this adventure be too much for James, Josh, and Sam.

James Thompson has another dream from the past, the furthest he's ever been in any of his dream, this time it's when Ian's Peak was first discovered by Dr. Ian Peak and a group of settlement back in 1860. Men were dying from an unknown illness and there didn't seem to be any cure. Nurse Yvonne has all the answer to this great mystery of all. James realised that the nurse from over a century ago was the spitting image of a nurse that's working at Ian's Peak hospital today. How could that be?

Was there a connection? Did the past had anything to do with what is happening in 2023 in Ian's Peak?

Find out with the next great mystery and see how it all end!

9 798987 274552